The TINKLERS THREE

Blame it on the Boo-gie
published in 2014 by
Hardie Grant Egmont
Ground Floor, Building 1, 658 Church Street
Richmond, Victoria 3121, Australia
www.hardiegrantegmont.com.au

A CiP record for this title is available from the National Library of Australia.

Text copyright © 2014 MC Badger
Illustration copyright © 2014 Jon Davis
Series design copyright © 2013 Hardie Grant Egmont

Design by Elissa Webb
Illustrations by Jon Davis
based on original characters by Leigh Brown
Typeset by Ektavo

Printed in Australia by Griffin Press, an Accredited ISO AS/NZS
14001:2004 Environmental Management System printer.

1 3 5 7 9 10 8 6 4 2

The paper this book is printed on is certified against the
Forest Stewardship Council® Standards. Griffin Press holds
FSC chain of custody certification SGS-COC-005088. FSC
promotes environmentally responsible, socially beneficial
and economically viable management of the world's forests.

THE TINKLERS THREE

BLAME it on the BOO-GIE

M·C·BADGER

illustrated by
jon davis

hardie grant EGMONT

CHAPTER ONE

ONE WINDY Monday morning, Marcus, Mila and Turtle Tinkler were going up the stairs to their flat. They lived on the thirty-third floor of thirty-three Rushby Road, which meant that there were a lot of stairs. They could have caught the lift but they had a rule:

> The TINKLERS never catch the LIFT on WINDY MONDAY mornings.

Each of the Tinklers was climbing the stairs in his or her own way. Turtle was crawling up the stairs. This wasn't because she couldn't walk. She could walk very well. It was because she thought she was a turtle. She had a red cardboard box tied to her back. This was her shell.

'Turtles LOVE climbing stairs,' she said. (Maybe you have guessed that Turtle has some strange ideas about turtles.)

Marcus Tinkler was climbing the stairs by walking on his hands. His older sister Mila was trying to walk up on her hands too. The only problem was she kept walking on Marcus's hands instead.

'It is not my fault!' said Mila. 'The problem is your hands are too big, Marcus.

You need to invent something to make them shrink.'

Marcus was good at inventing things. But he didn't think he could invent something to shrink hands.

'My hands aren't too big,' he said. 'You just need to practise.'

Maybe all of this sounds a little bit unusual to you. But none of it was at all unusual for the Tinklers. They were used to doing things differently from everyone else. They even had a rule about it.

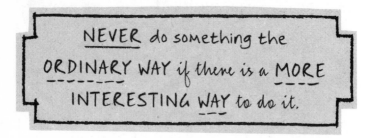

NEVER do something the ORDINARY WAY if there is a MORE INTERESTING WAY to do it.

The Tinklers' parents did things differently from other parents too.

They both worked in a travelling circus and were often away from home.

Marcus, Mila and Turtle planned to join their parents in the circus one day. But for now, they lived all by themselves, which meant they got to do things their own way.

Marcus was counting in Swedish as he went up the steps. He was trying to learn a new language every week.

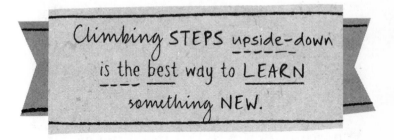

Climbing STEPS upside-down is the best way to LEARN something NEW.

At least, that was what Mila said.

The problem was that Swedish is very *HARD*.

So far, Marcus only knew a few words. He had learnt how to count to five, but he could only walk up three steps on his hands before he fell over.

Mila and Turtle were having trouble too. Mila could only walk up one step before she fell. And Turtle kept slipping backwards. By the time the Tinklers reached the twelfth floor of their building they all needed a rest.

Marcus went and leant against the door of flat number twelve. Turtle crawled up beside him.

Mila didn't sit down. She looked at the front door of flat number twelve and shivered.

'That flat gives me the CREEPS,' she said.

Marcus was surprised. 'Why?'

'Well,' said Mila, 'how long ago did the Petersons move out of it?'

The Petersons were the couple who used to live in flat twelve. Mrs Peterson liked to knit socks. Mr Peterson liked to make picture frames out of wood. Whenever the Petersons saw the Tinklers they would give them more socks and another picture frame.

The Petersons were very nice but Marcus had been a little bit glad when they moved out. They didn't need any more socks. And there wasn't any more room on their walls for picture frames.

'They moved out three months ago,' said Marcus. 'It's been empty ever since.'

'Exactly!' said Mila. 'That flat has been empty all that time, and no ghosts have moved in!'

'Why would we want ghosts to move into our building?' asked Turtle. 'Ghosts are very annoying. They float around all the time and get in your way. And they are so noisy with all that WHOO-ING! that they do.'

'Ghosts aren't real anyway,' said Marcus.

Mila didn't seem to hear Marcus. 'Look, I don't really want ghosts in here either,' she said to Turtle. 'But I don't want to break the law.'

'What law?' asked Marcus.

Mila knew a lot about rules and laws. The only thing was that Marcus sometimes got the feeling she made them up.

'It's against the law for a place to be empty for more than three weeks without a ghost moving in. We could get into big trouble if the police find out.'

'Well, how do you know that no ghosts have moved in?' Marcus asked. 'Maybe they are in there, hiding.'

He was joking. He knew there were no such things as ghosts.

But Mila didn't think it was a joke. She jumped to her feet. 'You're right, Marcus!' she said. 'We'd better go in and check.'

CHAPTER TWO

MILA HURRIED OVER to the door.

'Quick!' she said to Marcus. 'Give me your **skeleton** key.'

A couple of weeks ago Marcus had made a special key in his workshop. This key could open any door. Keys like this are called skeleton keys. But Marcus's key was a skeleton key for another reason too. It was shaped like a skeleton.

'We don't need to use it,' said Marcus.

'The Petersons gave us their spare key.'

'We should use the skeleton key anyway,' said Mila. 'That way, the ghosts will know that this is a good place for them to stay.'

'Well, OK,' said Marcus. Secretly he was happy to use his new invention! Marcus took the skeleton key out of his pocket and went over to the door of flat number twelve. He put the key into the lock and turned it.

The door silently opened.

Mila gasped.

'Did you hear that?' she asked.

'No,' said Marcus and Turtle.

'Exactly!' said Mila. 'The door didn't CREAK one tiny bit. Ghosts really hate quiet doors.'

The Tinklers Three went into the Petersons' old flat. It was totally empty. There weren't even any blinds on the windows. Sunlight streamed in.

'Look at this place!' said Mila. She sounded disgusted. 'No wonder there are no ghosts in here. It is way too bright and clean!'

'Ghosts like dark corners to hide in. They like window shutters that BANG. They like spiders' webs and bats. They like chocolate ice-cream.'

'Are you sure ghosts like chocolate ice-cream?' said Marcus. 'I've never heard that before.'

Mila grinned. 'Well, I like chocolate ice-cream,' she said. 'It helps me think. That's because it keeps my brain nice and cool. Brains work best when they are cool. Let's go home and have some chocolate ice-cream. Then we can make a plan. We need to get some ghosts into this place. If we don't, we will be in really big trouble.'

When the Tinklers got back to their flat on the thirty-third floor they each had a job to do.

Marcus's job was to feed the pigeons. He did this every day. Sometimes he used a grabby hand to feed them. This was one of his inventions. It was a stick with a grabber on the end.

Marcus would put bread in the grabby hand. He got the bread from the bakers who lived on the ground floor.

Then he would hold the stick out the window. The pigeons would fly past and eat the bread.

But sometimes the pigeons just waited on the window ledge to be fed.

Turtle's job was to take off her red box and put on a blue one. The red one was her outdoor shell. The blue one was her indoor shell.

Mila's job was to get the chocolate ice-cream. She also got two bowls and two spoons. One was for her and one was for Marcus. For Turtle, she got a bowl of lettuce.

Once they had finished their jobs they met up in the kitchen. Mila put the bowls of ice-cream and the lettuce under the kitchen table. This was because they had a rule:

You MUST always eat UNDER the table in OCTOBER!

The Tinklers sat on some books under the table. There were a lot of books under the kitchen table, because of another rule:

YOU MUST READ books UNDER the table on MONDAYS.

When the Tinklers weren't reading the books, they used them as little chairs.

When all three Tinklers were sitting under the table, Mila banged her spoon on the side of her ice-cream bowl.

'Let's have a meeting,' she said. 'We need to get some ghosts to move into flat number twelve. Any ideas?'

'We should put a lettuce leaf outside the building,' said Turtle. 'Then we should put another one just inside the building. Then we should keep putting leaves on every step leading right to the door of number twelve.'

Mila shook her head. 'That won't get ghosts,' she said. 'That will get turtles.'

Then Marcus had an idea. 'Ghosts like dark places, right?' he said.

Mila nodded. 'They also like lights that flash **ON** and **OFF**. They like *HIGH* screaming noises. They also like low rumbles. They like SMOOTH floors so they can glide around. Ghosts love gliding.'

Suddenly Mila SNEEZED. She always did this when she had an idea.

'I know just what we should do!' Mila said. She looked very excited. Her face had gone all red. Her eyes were bright.

'What?' said Marcus.

'Let's throw a GHOST disco PARTY! There are flashing lights at a disco. And music that screams and rumbles. The ghosts will L O V E it.'

Marcus wasn't sure about this. 'I've never heard of a ghost disco party before,' he said.

'Of course you haven't,' said Mila. 'I only just invented it. But it's a very good idea, don't you think? Lots of ghosts will come. And I'm sure that some of them will decide to stay.'

CHAPTER THREE

'A GHOST DISCO is a great idea,' said Marcus. 'Everyone knows that ghosts like to dance.'

'They do?' Mila was surprised that Marcus knew anything about ghosts.

'Of course!' said Marcus. He grinned. 'They love to get down and <u>boo</u>-gie.'

'Who told you that?' asked Mila.

'I read it in here,' said Marcus.

He patted the book he was sitting on. 'It's a fact book about ghosts.'

'Let me see!' said Mila. She pulled the book out from under Marcus and looked at it.

'This isn't a *fact* book about ghosts,' she said. 'It's a *joke* book about ghosts.'

'Really?' said Marcus. He pretended to be surprised.

'Yes, really,' said Mila. She turned the book around. 'See? It's called One Hundred Ghastly Ghost Jokes for Boys and Ghouls.'

Marcus shrugged. 'OK, it *is* a joke book,' he said, 'but I've still learnt a lot of useful things from it.'

Mila looked curious. 'Like what?'

'Well,' said Marcus, 'I know where ghosts post their letters.'

'Where?'

'At the ghost office!' said Marcus. 'And they buy their food at the ghostery store.'

Mila groaned. 'I think I'm going to get sick of your ghost jokes very soon.'

'Don't worry,' said Marcus. 'I only have ninety-eight more to go.'

Mila got a notepad out from the pile of books she was sitting on. She picked up one of her plaits and pushed a pencil out of the end. Mila said that — plaits were the BEST place to keep PENCILS. — That way you never forgot them.

'Let's make a to-do list,' Mila said. 'Should we have the disco tomorrow?'

Marcus shook his head. 'No, let's have it tonight.'

'Why?' asked Mila.

'Because today is Moanday. That is the best day for a ghost disco.'

'That's a bad joke,' said Mila, 'but it's a good idea. We'll have the disco tonight.'

Mila scribbled in her notebook with her plait-pencil.

'We'll need spiders,' she said. '*Lots* of spiders. We'll let them loose in the Petersons' flat and they can build webs in there. Ghosts love spider webs. Who wants to collect some spiders?'

'No, thanks,' said Marcus. He didn't really like spiders.

Mila sighed. 'OK then, I'll get them,' she said. 'I'm not scared.'

'You're not scared?' said Marcus, grinning. 'I'd better get some scare spray then!'

'No more jokes!' said Mila. She grabbed the joke book. She went over to the window and opened it. All the pigeons looked up.

'Coo coo?' they said.

The Tinklers understood a bit of bird language. Mila knew that this meant 'Do you have seed bread for us?'

'I do have seed bread for you,' said Mila. 'But first you must do something for me.'

She put the book on the window ledge. 'Take this book and drop it into a lake somewhere. Then I'll give you all the seed bread you can eat.'

'Coo coo!' said the pigeons. That meant 'Get the seed bread ready. We'll be back soon.'

Two pigeons grabbed the book from the top. Two more grabbed the book from the bottom. Together they flew off with the book.

Marcus was a bit sorry to see the book go, but he decided it didn't really matter too much.

Mila crawled back under the table.

'OK, then,' she said. 'Let's get on with our disco plans. Where is my to-do list?'

'Can't you find it, Mila?' said Marcus.

'No,' said Mila, looking all around.

'Then maybe you need tacles,' said Marcus.

That's why Marcus wasn't worried about losing his book. He knew all the jokes off by heart anyway.

★ ★ ★

CHAPTER FOUR

MILA LEFT TO collect some spiders.

'While I'm gone, you and Turtle need to make the Petersons' flat dark,' she said to Marcus. 'No ghosts would ever be seen in such a bright place.'

Marcus and Turtle went to look for something they could use to cover the windows in flat number twelve.

'We could put up some blankets over the windows,' suggested Marcus.

But then he remembered they didn't have blankets anymore. The day before they had been in the park. They had seen lots of possums there.

'They look *COLD*,' Mila had said. 'Let's give them some blankets.'

So the Tinklers had gone home and cut head holes in their big blankets. Then they had gone and given them to the possums.

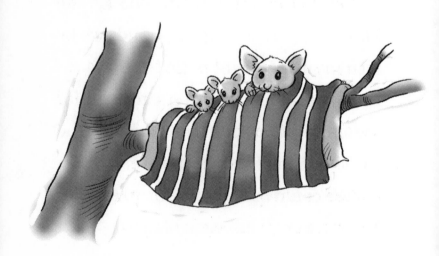

* * *

'We could paint the windows black,' suggested Turtle.

'Good idea,' said Marcus. 'Except we don't have any black paint left.'

The Tinklers had used up all their black paint the week before. They had painted their bathroom black so they could all pretend they were in outer space.

'That's true,' said Turtle. 'What do we have?'

'Boxes,' said Marcus. 'We have lots of boxes. Maybe we can cut some up and use them to block up the windows.'

'Those aren't boxes!' said Turtle. She looked worried. 'Those are my *shells*. You can't cut them up.'

'Why do you need so many shells, anyway?' asked Marcus.

'They are all different. One is my sleeping shell. One is my rainy day shell.'

Turtle picked up a bright pink box that was covered in glitter. 'And this one is my party shell.'

'And what about that one?' asked Marcus. He pointed to a box with bits of silver foil stuck to it.

'That is my spacesuit shell,' said Turtle. 'Turtles love to go into outer space.'

Marcus didn't bother to argue. There was no point. Also he had just had an IDEA.

'We have a lot of socks,' he said. 'Maybe we could stick those on the windows in flat number twelve?'

'That is your best idea ever,' said Turtle. 'I will go and find some glue.'

Marcus didn't think it really was his best idea ever. He had a feeling that Turtle was just glad he wasn't going to use her boxes.

'OK,' he said. 'I'll collect the socks.'

Marcus and Turtle took the glue and the socks to flat twelve. Then they got to work. Marcus put glue on the windows. Turtle stuck the socks on.

'This is fun,' said Turtle. 'It's a bit like doing a *JIGSAW PUZZLE* where every piece is shaped like a sock.'

The door opened and Mila came into the flat, looking very proud.

'Look at all the spiders I collected!' she said. 'I got the *SCARIEST* ones of all. They are red with black spots.' She held up a big glass jar.

Marcus looked into it. 'Those aren't spiders,' he said, 'They're *ladybirds*.'

Mila frowned. 'You're wrong. They're black spot spiders,' she said. 'They're the most deadly spiders in the world.'

'Mila,' said Marcus, 'they only have six legs. Spiders have eight.'

'These ones used to have eight legs,' Mila said. 'But they lost a few in fights with other spiders.'

'Sometimes,' said Marcus, 'I feel like the only normal one in this family.'

'You're *so* not normal,' said Mila. 'You're sticking socks to the window.'

'That's true,' Marcus agreed. 'But it's doing a good job of making the room dark, don't you think?'

When all the windows were covered with socks, Mila looked around.

'We need to do some MESSING UP,' she said. 'This place is way too clean.'

She went to the front door and opened it. Outside were some big plastic bags.

'What's in the bags?' asked Marcus.

'This one's full of dust,' said Mila, picking up a bag. 'And that one's full of leaves and old dirty paper. We need to spread this stuff all around to make this place nice and messy.'

Messing up is much more fun than tidying up. The Tinklers Three sprinkled the dirt and dust on the floor. They stuck leaves and paper on the walls with glue. Marcus even found a spider in one of the bags. This time it was a real one. It crawled off into a corner and started spinning a WEB.

When the plastic bags were empty, Mila put on some white gloves.

'I'm going to check that we have made this flat good and dirty,' she said.

She ran a finger along one of the window ledges. Then she inspected her finger. The tip of the white glove was completely black with dust.

'Perfect!' said Mila. She looked pleased. 'That is just how ghosts like it.'

CHAPTER Five

MARCUS THOUGHT of something.

'How will the ghosts know about the disco?'

'Hmm,' said Mila. 'That's a good question.'

'We should make posters,' said Turtle. 'Then we can stick them up in places where we think ghosts might go during the day.'

'I know where ghosts go during the day,' said Marcus. He was grinning.

'Where?' asked Mila.

'They go to day_scare_ centres.'

'I know where ghosts really go during the day,' Mila said seriously. 'They go to laundromats.'

Marcus frowned. 'Why would they go there?'

'Have you ever seen a ghost in a dirty sheet?' asked Mila.

'No,' said Marcus.

'That's because they wash them every day,' said Mila.

'I've never seen a ghost in a clean sheet either,' Marcus pointed out. 'I've never seen a ghost at all. You know why? Because ghosts *don't* exist.'

'Just wait until our disco, Marcus,' said Mila. 'Then you'll see.'

'Let's make the posters for the ghost disco,' said Mila.

She found some old paper and colouring pencils, and the Tinklers sat on the floor to make some posters.

Mila's poster said:

GHOST DISCO! TONIGHT ONLY.

Marcus's poster said:

DO YOU HAVE *NO BODY* TO DANCE WITH? THEN COME TO OUR DISCO!

Then at the bottom in small letters he wrote: *BUT ONLY IF YOU ARE REAL.*

Turtle's poster said:

GHOST DISCO
AT THIRTY-THREE RUSHBY ROAD.

Then she drew turtles around the edge, using a white pencil.

'I'm drawing ghost turtles,' she explained.

When the posters were finished, the Tinklers went out to put them up. They put up one inside the lift. They gave one to the bakers on the ground floor. Then they headed off down the street.

At number eighteen Rushby Road there was a laundromat. Before the bakers moved into their building, the Tinklers went there all the time. Not to wash clothes, but to make cakes.

43

Mila said that — a <u>LAUNDRY</u> was the <u>BEST</u> place to make a <u>CAKE</u>. —

They would put flour, eggs, sugar, milk and butter into one of the washing machines and turn it on.

The washing machine would spin all the ingredients together to make the mixture. Then the Tinklers would take it home and bake it.

But the Tinklers didn't need to make cakes anymore. The bakers downstairs gave them all the cake they could ever need.

The Tinklers stuck up their posters in the laundry, then they headed towards home.

Mila was very pleased.

'I have a feeling there will be lots of ghosts at our disco tonight!' she said to Marcus and Turtle.

Then suddenly she stopped. 'We've forgotten the most important thing that we need for the disco!'

'What's that?' asked Marcus.

'Music, of course!' said Mila. 'The ghosts are going to need something to dance to.'

'We have lots of music on our computer,' said Marcus. 'We can use that.'

But Mila shook her head. 'No. That's *human* music,' she said. 'Ghosts don't like it. We need special ghost music.'

'What is ghost music?' asked Marcus.

'Well,' said Mila, 'it sounds a bit like the wind whistling through the trees. It also sounds like kids screaming on a roller-coaster. And it sounds like a hundred wolves howling.'

'Hmm,' said Marcus. 'I've never heard any music that sounds like that. Are you sure that ghosts won't dance to something else? What about ABBA? *Everyone* likes dancing to ABBA.'

'Not ghosts,' said Mila. 'Ghosts hate ABBA.'

'It's going to be very hard to find music that sounds like wind whistling, kids screaming and wolves howling,' said Marcus.

'Yes,' said Mila, 'it is going to be very hard. But I'm sure you will find something.'

CHAPTER SIX

THE TINKLERS OPENED the door to thirty-three Rushby Road and went inside. Straight away they heard a terrible noise. It was very *HIGH* but also very low. It sounded like a wail and a scream at the same time. And it was very, very loud.

'What's that noise?' asked Mila.

'I don't know,' said Turtle. 'But I don't

like it. It's hurting my ears.'

'Maybe it's something in the bakery?' said Marcus. 'Maybe they have a new machine for baking bread. A very noisy machine.'

Mila opened the bakery door to ask the bakers about the noise.

'We don't know what it is,' said the bakers. 'It's coming from upstairs.'

The Tinklers went to the stairs and listened. The bakers were right. The noise was coming from somewhere high in the building.

'I know what it is!' said Mila suddenly. 'It's ghosts! They saw our posters and they've come early for the disco. Marcus, you'd better go and find them. Tell them that the disco isn't ready yet. Tell them to come back later.'

'Me?' said Marcus. 'This was your idea. *You* should go and find them.'

'I'd love to,' said Mila. 'But I have to go and check on the spiders. I need to see if they are spinning webs or not. You're not scared, are you, Marcus?'

'I'm not scared of ghosts,' said Marcus. 'I'm scared of weird, loud noises.'

'I am not scared of ghosts or weird, loud noises,' said Turtle. 'I will go and see where it is coming from.'

'OK, I'll go with you,' said Marcus. He didn't want anyone to think that a turtle was braver than he was!

Slowly, Marcus and Turtle started walking up the stairs. On the fifth floor the noise was a bit louder. On the twelfth floor it was louder still. But when they got to the thirty-first floor it was the loudest of all.

Marcus and Turtle stopped. They looked at each other. 'This is the floor where the Splatley family lives.'

The Splatley family were Mr and Mrs Splatley and their three kids, called Sarah, Simon and Susie.

The Splatley children were the same age as the Tinklers, but that was the only thing they had in common.

For instance: Mila liked to eat chocolate ice-cream. Sarah liked to throw chocolate ice-cream out of the window at people walking down below.

Marcus liked to invent things. Simon liked to break things.

Turtle liked being a turtle. Susie liked being a pest.

See how different they were?

Marcus put his ear against the Splatleys' door. The horrible noise was definitely coming from in there.

'Maybe the Splatleys have trapped some ghosts in their house,' said Turtle. 'We had better check.'

Marcus didn't really think there were ghosts in there. But something was making that noise. What could it be?

Marcus took a deep breath. Then he knocked on the door.

Mr Splatley opened it.

'Hello, Marcus!' he said. Mr Splatley had a very high, squeaky voice. It was like the noise a dog toy makes when a dog CHEWS it.

'Hello, Mr Splatley,' said Marcus. 'Is everything OK in there?'

'Oh yes,' squeaked Mr Splatley. 'The kids are doing their singing practice. They have joined a choir.'

Marcus looked into the flat. Behind Mr Splatley he could see Sarah, Simon and Susie. Their mouths were moving up and down. The horrible noise was coming out of them. Their dog Fuzzby was sitting on the floor howling.

'Ah,' said Marcus. 'So that is what we could hear.'

Mr Splatley beamed. 'Don't they
sound great?'

'It's like nothing I've ever heard
before,' said Marcus, trying to be polite.

Turtle was not so polite. 'It sounds like a hundred trains running over a hundred cats' tails,' she said. 'No-one in the whole world would like that sound.'

Luckily she said it quietly.

Suddenly Marcus had an idea. 'We're having a disco tonight in flat number twelve,' he told Mr Splatley. 'Would Sarah, Simon and Susie like to come?'

Behind Mr Splatley, Marcus could see the three Splatley kids pulling horrible faces. But their dad didn't see them.

'I'm sure they'd love to come!' squeaked Mr Splatley. 'They have to go to choir practice tonight, but they could come to the party on the way.'

Marcus smiled. 'Great!' he said.

Mrs Splatley appeared at the door.

'Hello, Tinklers!' she said. She had a very loud, booming voice. 'You are just in time for a game of Ludo.'

Marcus took a big step backwards. Turtle took two. There was nothing the Tinklers HATED more than playing Ludo with the Splatleys.

'Sorry,' said Marcus. 'But we have to go and get ready for the disco.'

Then he and Turtle ran back down to the flat on the twelfth floor.

CHAPTER SEVEN

MARCUS AND TURTLE found Mila in the empty flat on the twelfth floor.

'I invited the Splatleys to the disco,' Marcus told her.

'Why did you do that?' said Mila.

'You know that scary sound we heard?' Marcus said.

'Yes,' said Mila.

'Well, that was the Splatleys singing!

59

I thought they could come and sing at the disco. I bet ghosts would love it,' said Marcus.

Mila thought about this. Then she nodded. 'You're right,' she said. 'Ghosts would like that music. It was a good idea to invite the Splatleys. Are you sure it wasn't my idea? I sneezed just before. You know that I always sneeze when I have an idea.'

'No,' said Marcus. 'It was definitely my idea. You were sneezing because it's dusty in here now.'

'Well, then,' said Mila, 'we're ready for the disco. The room is nice and messy. We have put up posters. We have music. And I've even put out some food and drink.'

Marcus looked around the flat. On the window ledge were some bowls and a few plastic cups. He picked up a cup and inspected it.

'These cups and bowls are EMPTY.'

'No,' said Mila. 'They're filled with AIR. That's what ghosts like to eat and drink. I made it all myself.'

'That's not what ghosts eat,' said Marcus.

Mila was surprised. 'What do they eat, then?'

'Spookghetti,' said Marcus, grinning. 'And for dessert they like I-scream.'

'Marcus, you don't know anything about ghosts,' said Mila. 'They like air.'

She took the plastic cup from Marcus and put it back on the window ledge.

'There,' she said, turning back to Marcus. 'Now we're ready. This is going to be such a GREAT disco party!'

Mila looked excited. Marcus could tell she was sure that ghosts would come to her party.

Marcus felt a bit sorry for her. She was going to be very disappointed when no ghosts showed up.

Suddenly, there was a strange noise. The Tinklers froze.

'What was that?' asked Mila.

'It sounded like someone tapping at the window,' said Marcus.

'And going "WHOO! WHOO!"' added Turtle.

'It must be some ghosts,' said Mila. 'They sometimes come to the window instead of up the stairs. You go and look, Marcus. I need to check on the spiders.'

Marcus peeled off one of the socks stuck to the window. He peeked out through the gap and saw six small ghosts floating outside the window. Marcus's heart was beating fast. He didn't believe in ghosts.

'Mila!' he said. 'Look! There are some little ghosts outside!'

Mila rushed over to see. The ghosts were wearing handkerchiefs instead of sheets.

'Let them in!' she said, opening the window.

The ghosts flew inside.

'Coo coo, coo coo,' they said.

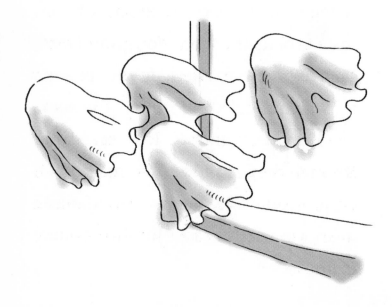

Marcus laughed when he realised what had happened.

'These are just pigeons,' he said. 'They must have flown through a washing line that was covered with white hankies.'

'Oh,' said Mila, disappointed. 'Well, it doesn't matter. They can eat seed bread in here so they make this place even messier.'

There was a knock at the door.

'That must be some *real* ghost guests!' said Mila. She hurried over to the door and opened it.

On the other side were the three Splatley kids. They were dressed in their choir costumes, which were long, white dresses that totally covered their normal clothes.

All that showed were their heads and the mean, grumpy looks on their faces.

'Good evening,' said Mila. 'Please come in and make yourselves at home.'

Marcus was surprised. Mila was not usually this polite to the Splatleys.

Sarah Splatley looked around the room. 'There's no-one else here,' she said.

'Not yet,' said Mila, still using her very polite voice. 'You're the first three ghosts to arrive.'

'Mila,' said Marcus. 'They aren't ghosts. It's the Splatleys.'

Mila rolled her eyes. 'Don't be silly, Marcus,' said Mila. 'Of course they're ghosts. Can't you see the long white sheets they are wearing? They have come to our disco.'

'No, they are definitely the Splatleys,' Marcus said.

He looked at the Splatleys. 'Tell her. And sing her one of your songs.'

The problem was that the Splatleys loved to disagree with people.

Simon Splatley shook his head. 'No, we're not the Splatleys. And we don't know how to sing.'

'See?' said Mila. 'I told you they weren't the Splatleys.'

Before Marcus could argue, there was another knock on the door. This time it was Barry and Betty, the bakers from downstairs. They were both covered in flour because they had been working hard all day.

'Hello, Tinklers,' said Barry. 'We saw your poster about the ghost disco.'

'So we brought you some snacks,' added Betty. She was holding a tray. It was full of muffins.

'Thanks,' said Marcus. He took the tray. 'What flavour muffins are these?'

Barry grinned. 'They are b̲o̲o̲berry, of course.'

'Of course!' Marcus grinned back. 'Good one.'

'I got the idea from a joke book that some pigeons dropped on our doorstep,' Barry explained. 'I gave them some seed bread to thank them for it.'

Marcus and the bakers were laughing when Mila came over to the door.

'More ghosts!' she said, still using her very polite voice. 'Please come in!'

'They're not ghosts,' said Marcus. 'They're the bakers from downstairs. They just have flour on them.'

But Mila didn't seem to hear him. She led the bakers into the room and gave them each a glass of air. 'We're so glad you could come,' she said. 'Lots of other ghosts will be here soon, too.'

'This is a stupid disco,' said Sarah Splatley.

'Yeah, it's boring,' added Simon.

Susie just stuck out her tongue.

'Well, why don't you start off the dancing?' said Mila. 'Then the other ghosts will join in.'

'But there's no music,' said Simon.

'Yes, that's a pity,' sighed Mila. 'We're waiting for the Splatleys. They are going to make the music for our disco. But they're not here yet. Maybe you could try dancing without music?'

Sarah Splatley opened her mouth to say something. Marcus knew she was going to say that Mila was silly and that it was impossible to dance without music.

But then something happened. One of the ladybirds Mila had collected crawled up the left leg of Sarah's jeans. At the same time, another ladybird crawled up her right leg. Two more climbed into the arms of her shirt.

The thing about ladybirds is that they are very TICKLY.

Sarah began to jump around. She kicked her legs out to the side, trying to get rid of the tickly feeling. She waved her arms around too. And she began to howl because the tickly feeling was so strong.

The Splatleys' dog Fuzzby ran into the flat and joined in the howling.

Simon and Susie Splatley always copied exactly what their big sister did. So when they saw her jumping around and heard her howling they did the same thing.

When the bakers saw the Splatleys jumping around, Betty had a good idea.

'Jumping around like that will get all this flour off us,' she said to Barry. So they joined in too.

Mila watched everyone leaping around.

'See, Marcus?' she said. 'I told you this would be a great disco party. I'm sure that one of these ghosts will decide to stay. Then flat twelve won't be unhaunted anymore.'

CHAPTER EIGHT

THE SPLATLEYS DIDN'T stay for very long. They left to go to choir practice. But the disco party didn't stop then. Marcus got the computer and put on ABBA. The bakers, the pigeons and the Tinklers Three kept on dancing.

At about nine o'clock, Mrs Fitz from floor thirty-two knocked on the door.

'What's all this noise?' she grumbled.

'I can hear it up in my flat.'

Mrs Fitz was a very nice lady but she pretended to be grumpy just to make the Tinklers happy.

'Hi, Mrs Fitz!' said Mila. 'Come in and join our party.' So Mrs Fitz did.

When the town hall clock struck **MIDNIGHT**, Mila stopped dancing. 'Isn't it past our bedtime?' she said.

'What are you talking about?' Marcus laughed. 'We DON'T have a bedtime.'

Mila laughed too. 'Oh yes. I forgot.' She started dancing again.

The pigeons went to sleep first. They lined up on the windowsill and closed their eyes.

Then the bakers left. 'Sorry we have to go,' they said, 'but we have to start baking again very soon.'

Mrs Fitz wanted to keep dancing all night but the Tinklers told her that it was time to go home. They had to be strict with her sometimes. Then finally the Tinklers went home to bed too.

★ ✷ ✦

Marcus was shaken awake by Mila the next day. This was very unusual. Usually Mila didn't wake up first. Sometimes she didn't wake up all day.

'What is it?' asked Marcus, sitting up.

'My plan worked!' said Mila. She sounded very excited. 'Some ghosts are moving into flat number twelve. Come and see!'

Marcus pulled on some clothes. Turtle pulled on a shell. Then the Tinklers Three went down to level twelve of their building. The door of the flat was open and two men were carrying a table inside. Behind him was another man carrying a lamp.

'You're right that some people are moving in, Mila,' said Marcus. 'But I don't think they're ghosts.'

'Just wait until you see the family,' said Mila. 'Then you will see I was right. Look! Here they come now!'

Marcus looked. Coming up the stairs were a family. There was a mother and a father. They were carrying cardboard boxes. There were also two children: a boy and a girl. All of them were very pale. They had pale skin and very fair hair. Their clothes were light too.

'See?' whispered Mila. 'They're a ghost family. I bet they like what we've done to the apartment.'

The Tinklers watched as the family looked around, confused, at the messy apartment and the socks stuck to the windows.

The mother said something to the children in another language.

'They're speaking a ghost language,' explained Mila confidently. 'It's called Spookish.'

Marcus listened carefully. And then he heard a word he recognised.

'Hang on. That's not Spookish,' said Marcus. 'It's Swedish! They're not ghosts, Mila.'

Just then the man dropped the box he was carrying. Out fell a pile of white sheets.

Mila gave Marcus a triumphant look. 'See?' she said. 'That proves it! Only a ghost family would have a box full of white sheets.'

Marcus sighed. Mila was hopeless!

'What do you think, Turtle?' he said. Maybe his younger sister would be a bit more sensible.

Turtle was staring at the man as he repacked the sheets.

'I think . . .' she said, 'I think that box would make a great shell.'

★ ★ ★

INTRODUCING
the TiNKLERS
THRee

MARCUS

Age: Eight.

How to spot him: He's the kid who is always collecting things to use in his inventions.

Favourite place to escape: His workshop in the basement.

Hobbies: Reading comics, swimming, going to the pet park, inventing things.

Biggest dream: He'd like to invent the world's best mailbox.

Dislikes: Adults who think the Tinklers need a grown-up to look after them.

Favourite food: Cheese and pineapple pancakes (he invented these himself!).

Biggest secret: He isn't sure he wants to join the circus like his parents. He thinks he might like to be an inventor instead.

MILA

Age: Ten.

How to spot her: She's the girl with a bird's nest on her head.

Likes: Making up new rules.

Dislikes: Playing Ludo with the Splatley family.

Biggest dream: To make a bed she could wear so she would never have to get up.

Thing that annoys her most: Ice-cream should come in bigger tubs (bathtub size would be perfect!).

Current project: Doing special arm exercises so she can learn to fly.

When she grows up: Mila can't wait to join the circus like her parents.

Favourite thing to cook: Upside-down cake. She makes it while hanging upside down.

TURTLE

Age: Three.

How to spot her: She's the kid with a box tied to her back.

Why is she called Turtle? Because she thinks she is one.

Favourite book: *Big Book of Turtle Facts* (written by Mila Tinkler).

Favourite food: Something that starts with 'L' and ends with 'ettuce'.

Favourite things to play with: Boxes and sticks.

She is smart because: She already knows how to read and uses lots of big words.

She is not so smart because: She thinks turtles can growl and fetch sticks.

When she grows up: She wants to be a shark.

the TINKLERS THREE

FOUR GREAT ADVENTURES!